THIS BOOK
BELONGS TO

This edition published by Parragon Books Ltd in 2015 and distributed by

Parragon Inc.
440 Park Avenue South, 13th Floor
New York, NY 10016
www.parragon.com

T#455377

ISBN 978-1-4748-3034-8

Printed in China

ALL ABOUT ME

PaRragon

Bath · New York · Cologne · Melbourne · Delhi
Hong Kong · Shenzhen · Singapore · Amsterdam

MARSHALL AND ME

Marshall the fire dog is a Dalmatian pup. He has white fur with black spots, and a little black nose.

What do you look like?
Draw or paste a picture
of you with Marshall.

RUFF-RUFF, RESCUE!

Marshall has blue eyes.
What color are your eyes? Check the right color below.

Brown

Blue

Green

Marshall wears a firefighter's hat.
What's your favorite thing to wear?
Draw it!

MARSHALL

GOOD FRIENDS

Chase the Police Dog pup is a natural leader and a great friend!

Chase wants to meet your friends! Write their names to finish these sentences.

.... is the sporty one.

.... tells the funniest jokes.

.... is the most caring.

.... is the best leader.

.... is the smart one.

I am the .... one!

My nose knows!

Draw or paste a picture of you and your friends.

FEELING BRAVE

When something needs to be dug, shoveled, or drilled, Rubble is the first on the scene! This pup is strong and brave when someone yelps for help.

Write names to finish the sentences.

The bravest person I can think of is ....

The strongest person I know is ....

Someone who would stay calm on patrol is ....

Which vehicle is Rubble's? Color it!

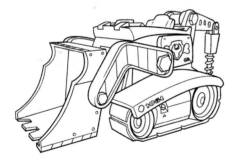

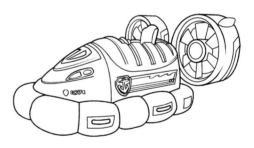

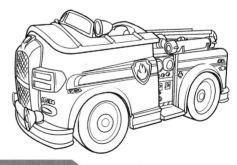

Draw a picture of you doing something really brave. It could be real or made up!

Here comes Rubble, on the double!

SMILEY SKYE

Nothing scares Skye! She's brave and very adventurous, and she loves to fly!

Check three words that describe you best.

- Brave
- Strong
- Helpful

- Shy
- Silly
- Happy

- Friendly
- Polite
- Kind

Trace the words!

Happy

Brave

Kind

Skye is smart and loyal, with a sweet smile. Draw faces to finish the sentences.

Yesterday, I felt

Today, I feel

Most of the time, I feel

Now color in Skye's wings. Pups away!

THINGS WE LIKE

Rocky the recycling pup can always find the right object to solve a problem!

Rocky is a great member of the team! He likes:

- **Recycling**
- **Playing ball**
- **Tools**
- **Eating treats**

Color in Rocky's recycling truck. Green means go!

Things I like:

....

....

....

....

Draw or paste a picture of something you like.

MAKING A SPLASH

Zuma is the team's water-rescue dog. He loves to spend time on the beach, so he can go surfing and diving.

Have you ever been to the beach?

Yes   **No**

Where would you like to go on vacation?

....

How would you like to get there? Check your choice.

By car   **By train**

On a boat   **On a plane**

By helicopter

18

Draw or paste a picture below of you on vacation.

What are you doing in the picture?

....

Ready, set, get wet!

RYDER HERE!

Do you have what it takes to help Ryder lead the PAW Patrol? Choose the right pup for the job.

There's trouble in the air. Do you send Skye or Rubble?

A ship is lost at sea. Do you choose Rocky or Zuma?

Oh no, there's a fire! Do you pick Marshall or Chase?

Draw a picture of your favorite PAW Patrol pup!

PAW Patrol—let's roll!

ME AND MY HOME

The PAW Patrol works hard to keep Adventure Bay safe.
Tell the pups all about your home.

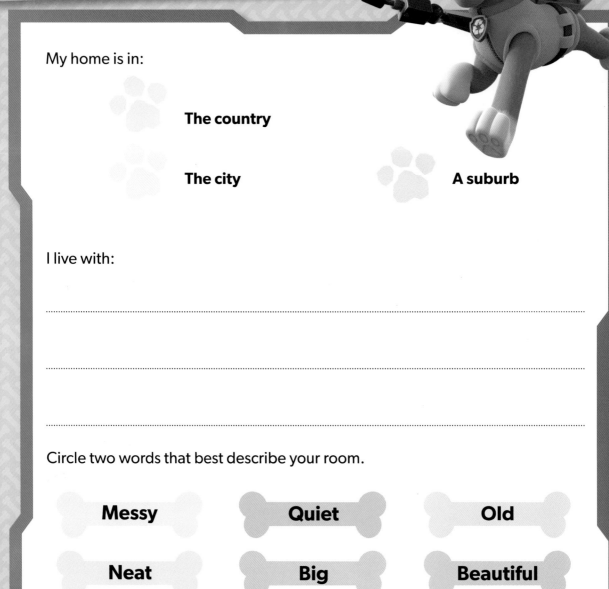

My home is in:

The country

The city   **A suburb**

I live with:

....

....

....

Circle two words that best describe your room.

Messy	**Quiet**	**Old**
Neat	**Big**	**Beautiful**
Noisy	**Small**	**Happy**

- Draw or paste a picture of your home.

  What do you like about where you live?

  ....

WHAT A TREAT!

When their work is done, the off-duty doggies always get a pawsome treat! Sometimes they get a special snack and other times they play at Pup Park. What are your favorite treats? How do you like to spend your free time?

Choose one answer for each sentence.

My favorite snack is:

- String cheese
- Grapes
- Pretzels

My favorite reward is:

- A gold star
- A trophy
- A certificate

On my birthday, my favorite thing is:

- A big present
- A giant cake
- A party

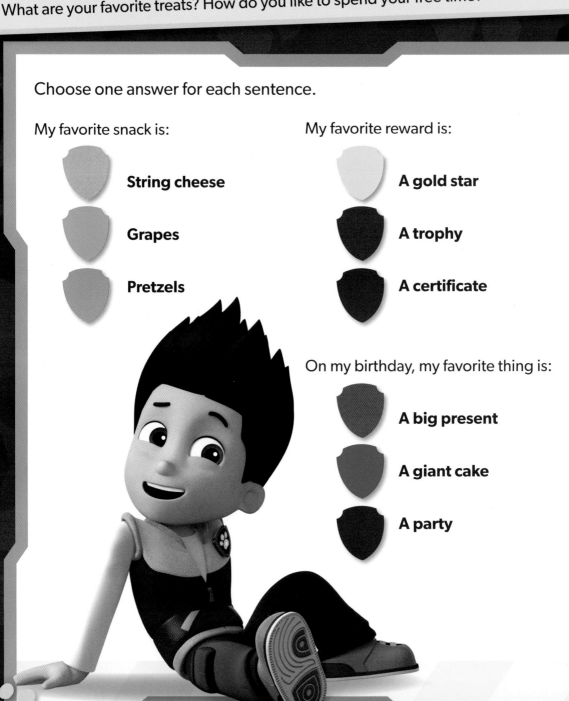

Fill the paw prints with drawings of your favorite treats.

THINGS I LIKE TO DO

Rocky loves to collect things as a hobby, while Marshall can't resist playing with a ball! What are your favorite things to do?

Draw a picture of you doing something that you love to do!

What are you doing in the picture?

....

You get to pick a new hobby! What is it?

Swimming

Riding horses

Playing an instrument

Collecting something

Trampolining

Racing bikes

Which friend would you pick to share your new hobby with?

....

....

....

....

I'M FIRED UP!

MY FAVORITES

Skye's favorite game is Pup Pup Boogie, while Rubble loves nothing more than a warm bath at Katie's Pet Parlor! What are your favorite things?

Circle your favorite color.

Choose your favorite badge.

Pick your favorite shape.

Write the name or draw or paste a picture of each of your favorite things.

Favorite game

Favorite book

Favorite place

Favorite toy

Favorite animal

This pup's gotta boogie!

THINGS I'M GOOD AT

Chase has a talent for sniffing out clues! He's also good at directing traffic and blocking off dangerous roads.

Draw circles around the things that you're good at doing.

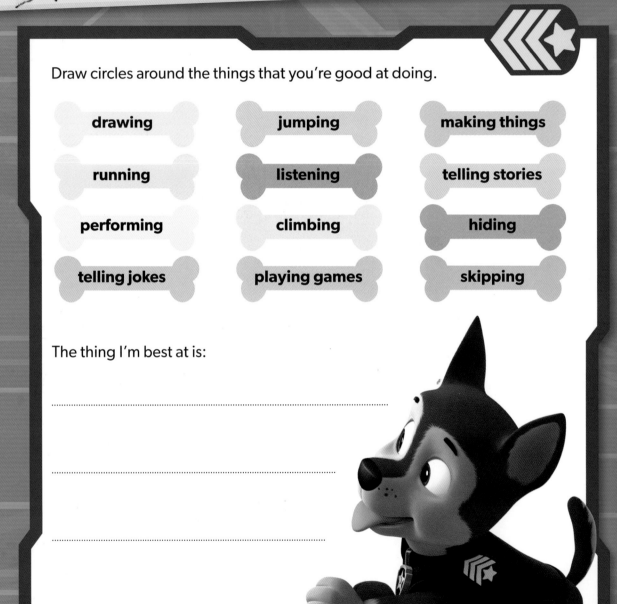

drawing

jumping

making things

running

listening

telling stories

performing

climbing

hiding

telling jokes

playing games

skipping

The thing I'm best at is:

....

....

....

....

....

Chase is on the case with his searchlight! Add some color so he's ready for action.

31

WORKING TOGETHER

Zuma loves helping people! Draw or paste a picture of a time when you've solved a problem, or worked as part of a team with your friends.

If you and your friends formed your own team like the PAW Patrol, what would it be called?

....

What job or special skill would each member of your team have?

My job or special skill: ....

Friend 1
Name: ....

Job or special skill: ....

Friend 2
Name: ....

Job or special skill: ....

Friend 3
Name: ....

Job or special skill: ....

Friend 4
Name: ....

Job or special skill: ....

MY ADVENTURES

Ryder is calling the pups to their next adventure.
PAW Patrol!—to the Lookout!

Color in the Lookout
so the pups can find it.

What adventures have you been on? Write about a real or imaginary adventure!

Where did the adventure happen?

....

....

Who was there?

....

....

What happened?

....

....

How did you feel?

 Excited   **Frightened**   **Brave**

MORE ADVENTURES

You're going on an adventure with the PAW Patrol! Will you travel in Rubble's digger, or Zuma's hovercraft? In Marshall's fire engine, or on Ryder's quad bike?

Color the vehicle you would most like to travel in.

Design a new vehicle for the PAW Patrol and draw it here.

Who will drive your special vehicle? Draw a circle around the driver.

No job is too big, no pup is too small!

BIRTHDAY FUN

Whenever it's a pup's birthday, the PAW Patrol celebrates with gifts and a paw-some party. Tell them all about your last birthday!

How old did you turn?

I turned .... years old.

What gifts did you get? ....

....

....

....

Draw or paste your
favorite party pictures!

PARTY PUPS

Now let the PAW Patrol pups help you plan the paw-fect party for your next birthday!

Theme: ....

Food: ....

....

Guests: ....

....

Songs: ....

....

....

Draw or paste a picture of your dream birthday cake.

What flavor is it?

My cake is .... flavor.

IN THE PUP PACKS

Each member of PAW Patrol has a Pup Pack, where they keep the gadgets they need to save the day.

In Marshall's Pup Pack:

A double-spray fire hose.

In Chase's Pup Pack:

A flashlight, a megaphone, and a net.

In Rubble's Pup Pack:

A bucket-arm scoop.

In Rocky's Pup Pack:

A mechanical claw, a screwdriver, and lots of tools.

In Skye's Pup Pack:

A set of wings.

In Zuma's Pup Pack:

Air tanks and propellers.

Imagine that you had your very own Pup Pack. What would you put inside it? Draw it here!

PAW-SOME HQ

PAW Patrol HQ is in the Lookout, overlooking Adventure Bay.

If you and your friends had an HQ, where would you like it to be?

 In a treehouse

 In an igloo

 On a boat

 In a tent

 In a castle

 At the top of a tower

Outside HQ

Inside HQ

44

Now design your own HQ here!
Think about all the paw-some things you could have inside....

Outside HQ

Inside HQ